BIRTH RITE

A world of sex, magic and old gods awaits and the LaMascares Mansion is the doorway …

Justin Devereaux has always been different, and not just in looks from his parents. His interests run to the magical and mysterious while theirs seem very pedestrian and small. The one thing that has always interested him and frightened them is the LaMascares Mansion. The mansion has sat long, seemingly empty and abandoned, but Justin feels someone in it watching over him.

Peren LaMascares has been trapped in the mansion on the hill for too many years to count. He needs a LaMascares' heir to free him and bring about the family's – and world's – dark destiny. He finds that heir in the innocent, unsuspecting Justin.

Peren leads Justin into a world of sex, magic and old gods. Will Justin abandon all the morals he's ever had so that he can have the lust-filled passion that Peren offers forever?

BIRTH RITE

A RAYTHE REIGN NOVEL
by X. Aratare

Story by X. Aratare

Cover Illustration by Mathia Arkoniel

If you would like to see more of Raythe Reign Publishing, Inc.'s offerings please go to:

www.RaytheReign.com

BIRTH RITE

X. Aratare
STORY

Mathia Arkoniel
COVER ART

CHAPTER 1

BREAKING RULES

The house on the hill haunted Justin Devereaux. He could see the aged Victorian out of his bedroom window. Every night he watched the sun sink behind its hulking frame. The house looked to be on fire as the last rays of the sun hit it. He held his breath until the sun disappeared over the horizon and the house vanished into the gloom of night. He didn't feel completely at ease until he saw the house in the morning light and confirmed that it had not been burned away or swallowed by darkness forever. The house was known as the LaMascares Mansion though no LaMascares -- or anyone else -- had lived there during Justin's lifetime.

Even though Justin was eighteen, he had never set foot on the hill. Almost every other boy in town had braved the yard of the abandoned house. They ran up to the door, rang the rusted bell, and rushed off again. They laughed and hollered about how tough and brave they were. No one mentioned that all of them were white as sheets for hours after their adventures. Justin had never even been tempted to do what they did. Not because he was afraid of the house, in fact, he felt a strange kinship with it, but because he also respected the house and playing ding dong ditch seemed disrespectful.

Though the house had been abandoned as long as Justin had been alive, its shutters still hung straight despite the long winters. The gray paint remained fresh and did not peel even after the spring's lashing rains. It stood perfectly composed and still as stone. Yet somehow it gave off the impression of vibrant life behind its curtained windows.

"It's not empty, you know," Ellen Shafer, his best friend, had told him one day.

"I'm sure the rats are happy you're counting them as life." His eyes had drifted up toward the house. It loomed over the north half of Winter Haven like a raven on a perch. He had asked too casually then, "Are new people moving in or something?"

Justin's chest had clenched at the thought of people living in the house. They wouldn't belong. They would be trespassers. He had been surprised at his own vociferous feelings about it. He had never known the LaMascares and yet, he felt like if anyone should live in that house, it should be them.

"No, nothing like that." Ellen had paused. Her gaze had slid up to the house and then away. "But can't you feel the house watching us? It's always watching and I wonder what it intends to do."

And that image of the house watching all of them out of its graceful windows stayed with him. Unlike Ellen, Justin felt comforted by it, because it made him feel protected as if the house were a second set of parents or an old friend that was looking out for him. But that all changed at 4:30 p.m. one day in the fall while he and Ellen were walking home from high school.

"There are tunnels from the house on the hill to each and every one of our homes," Ellen said suddenly. She tucked a stray bit of brown hair behind her ear.

"Wait. What?" Justin skidded to a stop and turned to face her. He couldn't have heard her correctly.

"The hill is *riddled* with them. Like Swiss cheese," she said.

Justin let out an uncertain laugh. "Okay, that's a random conversation changer." They had been talking about the upcoming calculus test. How did the LaMascares Mansion sneak into their conversation? Especially when he didn't bring it up! He was the obsessed one. Not Ellen. "So ... tunnels? From the house on the hill to our homes? How do you know that exactly?"

"I've wanted to tell you about it all day." She bit her lower lip, nibbling at the already chapped flesh. "But people kept coming up and interrupting us and then there wasn't enough time to really tell you everything. And now ..."

"Now?"

"It might be too late," she whispered.

"You're acting like there's some clock out there counting down to our doom." He tried to make his voice light and teasing, but she didn't crack a smile. She was serious. "What's the deal, El?"

"I just feel that I've missed some window of opportunity or something." She shook her head.

Justin stared at her for a long moment. They had been best friends since both were in diapers and her family had moved next store to his. Ellen was the sister he had never had. Even if he had liked girls, he knew he could never like Ellen as more than a friend. She was the one he confessed all his stuttering and stupid feelings *to*. She wasn't the one he had those feelings *for*.

It was the same for her. She was smart and focused. She was going to be a scientist and had already been accepted at MIT. Boyfriends, makeup, dresses and parties held absolutely no interest for her. The LaMascares Mansion held even less. He'd told her

9

about his fascination with the house and she'd expressed a passing interest in it, but nothing more than that because it had no bearing on her life plan. Until now. Ellen wasn't fanciful, but there was no joking lilt to her tone and her furrowed brow and dark eyes told him she really meant what she had said.

"Explain exactly what you mean about these tunnels." Justin didn't try to hide his disbelief nor his interest. He felt both disturbed and elated to think that there was a physical connection between the Victorian and his own home, even if it was a dark, dank tunnel. "Because, uh, El, I don't have any tunnels in my house. I think I would have noticed."

Ellen rolled her eyes at him. "The tunnels are *underground* and they come right up to the foundation walls, but they don't open into our homes. Well, they don't open up into *everybody's* homes, anyways." She bit her lip. "Not yet."

A trickle of unease went up Justin's spine and he hiked his backpack up higher onto his shoulders to stop the prickly sensation. He could sense the house behind them. He forced himself to look at Ellen instead of craning his neck around to see the last sliver of the Victorian's turret through the trees. Her pale brow was furrowed and her mouth was twisted into a frown.

"You're serious," he said, saying his internal thought about her demeanor aloud for the first time.

She nodded and rubbed her gloved hands together. "I've never been more serious."

"So tell me about these tunnels and what they have to do with the LaMascares Mansion," Justin said. He felt a stab of jealousy that Ellen knew this incredible thing about the house before he did, because if he and the house were connected -- like he sometimes thought they were -- why had Ellen discovered this amazing fact first?

"I didn't know the tunnels and the house were connected. Not until last night. But I was worried about telling you anyways, because, well … because you *do* like the house so much," she answered.

"That doesn't make sense. I'm just … *interested*. The house interests me. Of course, I'd want to know about something like this! Who wouldn't want to know about something like this? I mean secret tunnels make me think of pirate treasure or something," he said, keeping his voice light and airy despite her grim demeanor.

She stared at him for a long time as if weighing whether she could tell him how she knew these things. He shifted from foot to foot in annoyance. They were best friends. She shouldn't have secrets from him especially about the house. But her eyes reminded him of adult eyes. They reminded him of his grandmother's eyes. But his grandmother had gone through great trials in her eighty-six years of life and Ellen was just eighteen.

"I had to be sure," Ellen answered finally.

"Sure of what?" He resisted the childish urge to stamp his feet. Wouldn't she just speak plainly?

"That I'm right," she said. "It's a lot to handle. It's totally … nuts actually." She let out a soft laugh that wasn't mirthful at all. "What I'm about to say will probably make even you think I've lost my mind."

"I won't think that. I can handle it," he assured her. "Whatever it is. You can trust me, El."

"I know I can trust you." The wind blew harder then and she clamped one hand down on her hat to stop it from blowing off. Her scarf streamed out behind her like a crimson flag. "I just didn't trust myself."

When the wind let them speak again, he asked, "What's going on?"

Her mittened hand left her hat and tightened on the straps of her backpack. "You remember last summer when we had workmen over to fix the basement? The foundation had cracked and when it rained it would leak all over the place and there was this ... this *smell?*"

"I guess." Justin vaguely recalled men in orange and brown coveralls with names stitched on the pockets coming in and out of Ellen's house, but he hadn't really paid attention to them. He and Ellen had stayed out of the basement for a few weeks, but that was as much as the incident had touched him.

"The workmen said that one of the foundation's walls was actually bulging inwards like something had been *pushing* from the other side," she explained.

His brows drew together and he raised a hand to stop her from continuing on with her story. "Wait a minute. Pushing *in?*"

"Yeah." Ellen's face was suddenly paler in the weak fall light. "When they removed the concrete over that area, they found a tunnel leading right up to the foundation's walls."

"You found a tunnel leading to your house *last summer* and you didn't say anything until *now?*" Justin squawked. "El! I can't believe you! We spent everyday together this summer and you never said a word!"

They had swum in the local pool, gone to the beach, and hung out watching movies until the sun started to peek over the horizon. They'd even talked about the house. But she'd never said a word about any tunnel.

I remember her being quiet for a few days, but I thought she was depressed about her folks arguing so much. She snapped out of it though. That was when the workmen were there, I think. I'm not sure though.

"Like I said, I didn't realize that the tunnel was connected to the house on the hill. Not then," she said.

"But you didn't think a *tunnel* leading into your house would interest me? I admit I'm a little obsessed about the mansion, but I do have other interests," he said. "I'm positive I would have wanted to know about the tunnel."

"I know!" Her shoulders hunched forward. "I can't explain it! I would have told you, but I ... I *forgot*."

"How could you forget?"

"I don't know! I can remember wanting to tell you. I remember *intending* to tell you before we went to the movies one night. Only ... I didn't. The memory just went away and I forgot all about it." Her arms flapped at her sides. She looked angrier about it than he did. She didn't like things she couldn't explain and this was unexplainable.

"You don't forget things," he said slowly. "Especially not things like a tunnel leading into your house."

"I know! That's why it's all so -- so *wrong*!"

"So what happened with the tunnel?" he asked.

"That's where it gets even *weirder*."

"It's already pretty damned weird," Justin said.

Her eyes went distant as she remembered. "The tunnel was *huge*. It was tall as Dad and as round as a marble. The dirt was ... was *funny*. It wasn't soft. It was almost like baked clay." She paused. Her eyes seemed to go misty for a moment as she whispered, "It was *perfect*."

Justin frowned at her use of the word "perfect." She said it like it left a tart, yet pleasant, taste on her tongue, but nothing she had described so far about the tunnel would make him think that it was "perfect." It was strange and weird and perplexing. Not perfect.

"Did you go inside the tunnel?" Justin asked. The skin between his shoulder blades crawled as he imagined the tunnel's ceiling arching over her head and the thick, oppressive darkness surrounding her.

"No, Dad wouldn't let me," she said and Justin felt a wash of relief go through him. "The workmen did though."

"Where did it go? To the house on the hill? Is that how you know --"

"I don't know," she interrupted sharply then softened her tone. "I mean I didn't know. Not then. The workmen only went a little ways inside, maybe fifty feet or so. But then they came right back out. They said there was a ... a *smell*." Her nose wrinkled as if she smelled on the wind whatever they had scented months ago. "Sweet and a little ... *rotten*, maybe? I don't know. But the one guy who went down the tunnel further than the others came hustling back first. He was sweating and shaking. He kept babbling something in another language. I didn't understand what he was saying, but the other workmen did and they all went pale."

"They wouldn't tell you what he was saying"

She worried at her lower lip again. A bead of blood burst out from the cracked skin and she swiped at it with her mittened hand. She stared down at the red smear on her glove like it was unexpected. Still looking at the blood, she said, "They claimed that all he said was that the smell got to him, but I didn't believe them. He was a big guy. Muscled arms with a lot of tattoos running up and down them like sleeves. But he was scared. I don't think he'd ever been scared in his life. He ran out of our house after that."

Justin frowned. His own physique was small. "Dainty," his father, Jack Devereaux, had said with a laugh. He'd softened the insult with a ruffle of Justin's black hair, but the sting of his father's words still hurt, because Jack was a big sunny bear of a man. Justin looked nothing like him. But Justin knew for all his small size, he wasn't a coward. He knew that he wouldn't have run out of that tunnel like a scared child.

"No one else went into the tunnel again. The remaining workmen just patched up the hole as fast as they could. They scooped up everything they had taken out of it, the dirt, the concrete, the plaster, and they shoved it back in. Dad said they did a crappy job, but they wouldn't come back to fix it. Dad let it go, because they never asked for any money either," she said.

14

"They just up and left without getting paid?" Justin's eyes widened.

"They wouldn't even answer our phone calls after awhile," she said.

"Something happened more than just a bad smell in that tunnel," Justin guessed.

"They just got out of our house like they couldn't bear to stay another second. Like they were terrified to stay. Dad didn't want me going into the basement for a few months after that," she said. "Remember? We stayed at your house a lot more for the last month before school."

Justin shifted from foot to foot. He did remember that. He even vaguely remembered being confused why the basement where they had spent all their time before was suddenly off limits. But parents were weird. They got ideas into their heads and teenagers just had to roll with it. He had assumed it was one of those things. But now he realized that the reason for being barred from the basement was far weirder than a bug up a parent's butt. The story was disturbing, but why would something that happened months ago matter now? How could time be running out on a busted basement?

"So why tell me all this now?" he asked. "I mean I'm glad you're doing it. But … it's been months. Did you just remember the tunnel or something?"

"Or something." She swallowed hard. "The wall opened up again. Last night."

Justin froze. "What?"

Ellen started to fuss with her jacket, plucking at it as if picking off invisible lint. It was a nervous tick she'd developed as a child, but had long since banished. It was unnerving to see it back again. She didn't look at him as she talked. She stared ahead of her, unseeing.

"I was in the kitchen after Mom and Dad had gone to bed," she told him. "I was studying and got thirsty. I had the refrigerator open and then I heard a ... a *thunk*. Like something heavy falling down in the basement."

"And you went down there?" Justin guessed.

He and Ellen had watched enough horror movies together to know that the person who checked out sounds in a basement late at night ended up eaten by monsters. Based on these films, they had put together three main rules that they said they would observe at all times. Rule number one was never go into basements or attics after hearing a spooky sound, especially if alone. Rule number two was never run into the woods in shoes that would cause you to fall down. Rule number three was to never break rules number one or two.

"I know I broke the first rule," Ellen answered ruefully.

"Damned straight! El, you're lucky that the monsters didn't chow down on you for that!" He laughed, but his amusement dried up when she didn't join in.

"That's the thing, I didn't really believe that something bad could happen. I didn't believe in monsters, Justin." Her complexion was now white as snow.

Her words hung in the air like frost. The skin between Justin's shoulder blades twitched this time. She was speaking in the *past* tense. She clearly believed something different now.

Ellen believes in monsters? My scientist believes in dark, scary things?

"So what exactly *did* happen when you went into the basement?" he asked.

"I flipped on the light and went down the stairs. At first, nothing looked wrong, you know?" Her lips thinned as she pressed them together tightly. "But then there was another sound. More ... subtle? Like it wanted me to know that I hadn't imagined the first noise."

"Where was the sound coming from?" Justin held himself very still as if afraid any movement might scare her off from telling him the rest and he was suddenly very desperate to hear the rest.

16

"From beyond the washer and dryer. The space where all the old furniture is," she said. "I flipped on the lights as I went. I kept expecting them not to work, but they did. Even if they hadn't, I think I still would have gone forward. I -- I *had* to go see."

Justin felt the pull of the LaMascares Mansion at that moment. It was almost like a physical tug on his head, but he fought not to look. "What does this all have to do with the house on the hill?"

She raised one hand to stop him. "I'm getting to that. Just let me – let me tell it like I want to." She then whispered, "Like I *have* to."

"All right. All right. Tell it how you want to," he said, though he had to push down his need to get it all out of her right then and there.

"The workmen hadn't fill the hole with cement. After they tossed everything in, they had just bricked it up and smeared plaster over it. I don't think that's safe, but -- but that's what they did." She wrapped her arms around her torso. "When I got down there, I saw that a few bricks had fallen out or -- or had been *pushed* out."

Pushed. Jesus, when did 'push' start meaning 'scary as hell?'

"Which was it do you think? Pushed or fallen?" he asked.

Her gaze met his and she gave him a shaky smile. "Oh, pushed. Definitely pushed."

His tongue stuck to the roof of his mouth. "O—okay. Go on."

"The bricks were down on the ground. And there was this hole," she stopped.

Justin grabbed her arm gently. "Jesus, El. A -- a *hole*?"

She didn't answer him. She was lost in her story. "I went up to the hole. It was a little higher than my eye level. I got up on my tippy toes to look inside."

"El!" Justin's throat felt like it was closing up.

"I know." She gave out a high-pitched giggle that was so unlike her. She slapped a hand over her mouth as if to stuff it back in. "It was stupid, but I just had to."

"What did you see?" Justin felt like he did when he watched the sun go down behind the LaMascares Mansion: expectation mixed with formless anxiety.

"I didn't see anything. It's what I *heard.* I heard him," she answered. Her eyes glowed with this fervent, feverish look.

"Heard ... *him*?" Justin's voice shook.

"That's how I found out about the tunnels. He told me. He said that there's one connecting every house in Winter Haven to the LaMascares Mansion," she said. "There are miles of tunnels. Miles and miles through the dirt, through the dark."

"Are you saying that he's – he's ..." Justin's voice broke off. He didn't know what he meant to ask.

She answered calmly, "He said he traveled through the tunnels to my house. He said he came from the LaMascares Mansion. It's where he lives."

18

CHAPTER 2

THE LAST OF HER

*J*ustin forced himself not to shake Ellen again. How could she have been so very brave and so very stupid at the same time? Chasing after sounds in a basement? Looking into a hole? Talking to someone or, God, maybe *something* in a tunnel that simply shouldn't exist?

But at the same time, Justin felt a rush of something hot run through him. His heart beat faster and his palms sweated in his gloves. Anything that was in a tunnel like that had to be *otherworldly*. The man claimed to have come from the house on the hill. He claimed to have walked through a tunnel, underground, black as pitch, for over a mile and then stood at the foundation of Ellen's house. He had *pushed* bricks out to draw attention to himself. He hadn't called out, but let the clank of bricks landing on concrete speak for him. And then, he had simply stood there, waiting for Ellen to come find him. Who did that? Why would anyone do that?

19

It wasn't right. It wasn't normal. It was otherworldly. Justin knew it.

"His voice was so *amazing*, Justin. I felt like I was floating on it," she said and that dragged him out of his thoughts. "It reminded me of being on the ocean when the sky looks like it's going to storm, but the swells are still peaceful."

"James Earl Jones in a hole?" Justin joked, but it fell flat even to his ears.

Ellen nodded. "It was sensual. A bit like Vader's except without the heavy breathing."

"Wow, that's … something." Justin felt another stab of jealousy even as he was deeply disturbed and engaged by her story.

Justin could imagine the encounter with the mysterious man. He saw in his mind's eye the jagged hole in the wall. It would be dark inside. The smell of mildew and moistness would permeate the air. But then a dark as molasses, rich as summer honey voice would flow out of that blackness and everything would change.

Because no one like that could be ordinary. They'd have to be extraordinary. Justin mentally shook himself. *No, no, they would have to be weird and unnatural!*

Weird and unnatural that person might be, but his soul chafed at the fact that he was not the one to experience it. Why was she chosen to have this incredible encounter, even if it was scary? Why wasn't he chosen? He cared about the house! He had dreamed of meeting someone otherworldly all his young life. Ellen didn't even believe in those things! But she had been picked to experience this. It wasn't fair.

"They're finding new species in the rain forests every day. Perhaps vampires, fairies and other mythical beings like that do exist, but they just haven't been discovered yet," she had told him once when he had asked her if she these otherworldly beings could be real.

20

But Ellen had no passion for the otherworldly to be real. They either were or they weren't. She didn't desire them to exist. He knew that the discovery of a vampire would not inspire her any more than the discovery of a different species of butterfly.

"What was he like, El? What did he say? What did you see?" Justin asked, his questions nearly tripping over one another.

"He said he was glad to finally meet me. That it had been so long since he had talked to someone. He was lonely. So lonely." Her eyes went bleak. "He had been trapped within the house for almost two decades."

"Two decades?" This had Justin's mouth falling open both in shock and in sadness. All those days and nights he had looked over at the house, feeling that there was someone there, watching him, had likely been *true*. But this person had been trapped. If Justin had actually gone up to the house like the other boys would he had realized that someone was inside? Would he have been able to save this mystery man? Release him? Justin could have been a savior. But then he shook his head.

This makes no sense. How can someone be trapped within a house? It's not a prison. It would be easy to break out through a window if not a door. There are no bars on them. If he can walk through tunnels then he's not physically incapable of escaping.

She nodded. "He said … he's been *imprisoned* inside of the house for twenty years. But now … now he was breaking free."

"Imprisoned? But why? How? Who?"

"He wouldn't tell me. He just said that he had been wronged and needed help," she said.

"Of course, he needs help!" Justin turned, ready to march up to the house and break down the door to get to this man and free him. If he was being held prisoner, Justin wouldn't allow it to go on for even one more moment.

"No!" Ellen grabbed his arm to stop him. "No!"

21

"What do you mean 'no'? He's imprisoned, El, we can't let that go on --"

"What if he's *meant* to be? What if there's a *good* reason for it? You're not thinking right, Justin!" she cried.

"I'm the one not thinking right? El, you're the one allowing a man to be kept prisoner in a house!"

"Justin!" Her expression was fierce. "Think on what I've told you! He walks through tunnels -- tunnels that should not exist unless massive machines dug them, but we know that *no machines* have created them. We would have known about such a project and we don't! He stands in darkness and -- and whispers ..."

"It sounds weird and terrible and ... look, if he's been imprisoned for decades, he might not know how to act normally with people. " He shook his head. "But, El, that doesn't mean that he's a bad person --"

"He told me that he cannot walk outside. Not in the light of the sun or moon. Not yet. Just the tunnels. At least, for *now*," she said.

Justin blinked. "Why can't he walk out in the light?"

"He wouldn't say," she said simply and her hands rose and fell. "It was an insane conversation. It was an insane experience, but it happened and -- and I need to figure it out!"

Justin stared at her. Something otherworldly had made contact. Maybe the man was a vampire and couldn't bear the sun. *Or the moon?* Or maybe it was a magical spell that kept him within the house's walls unless he traveled through the earth. Or maybe -- Justin shook his head. He could speculate for a hundred years and never know the truth. He needed to talk to the man and find out for himself.

"I want to talk to him. Can we go to the LaMascares Mansion and speak to him now? If not, will he come back to your place? I can speak to him there," Justin said.

"This is why I didn't want to tell you about it!" she wailed.

"What? Why? Because you're afraid of him so I should be? El, this is -- this is world-shattering! This is awesome! I mean you're talking to someone ... well, someone not like the rest of us! It's amazing!" Justin enthused.

Ellen tugged at her hat as she thought about what he had said. "Justin, there must be a reason for why he's imprisoned in that house. We don't know why and I wouldn't trust anything he said. Don't you see that? Talking to him is just asking to be lied to."

"Not necessarily. El, if he's a vampire or -- or warlock or something, in the past people would have thought he was *evil*," Justin said. "But that's just prejudice and fear. Just because someone is imprisoned doesn't mean they should be."

"I knew you would say that. I knew you would feel that way." Her head tipped down and she clasped her hands together.

"Isn't it *logical* to feel that way?" he pressed her.

"If you had heard him, you would understand that *logic* has nothing to do with this. It's something I feel in the base of my spine. He's dangerous. Maybe even ... *evil*," she breathed out.

"Evil? You're kidding right? You talking about evil as if its a real, tangible thing instead of an outdated concept of --"

"I was wrong," she interrupted. "I was wrong and now I know that."

"Then let me talk to him and come to my own conclusions," he said mulishly.

"No."

"El!"

"No! Because that's exactly what he wants!" she shouted.

Silence fell between them as those words echoed in the still fall air.

Finally, he asked softly, "He wants to speak to me?"

"Yes," she said. Her shoulders sagged.

Justin shivered. It felt like an electric current went through him. He began to turn his head toward the house on the hill, but Ellen grasped his chin to keep him from looking at it.

"Don't! Don't look. Don't draw any more of his attention," she whispered.

"But -- but someone is really there! In the house and -- and he knows about me! All this time I've *felt* him! And you tell me he's been imprisoned and he wants to talk to *me*, but I just need to let it go?" Justin heard the almost star struck quality to his voice and tried to swallow it, but it wouldn't go down. "Is he a vampire? Or werewolf? Or sorcerer? Or who knows? He's something incredible! I feel it! You can't stop me from talking to him! You can't keep this to yourself!"

"That's just it! Listen to me! Listen to yourself!" she cried. She grabbed his arms and shook him just like he had envisioned shaking her.

"You talked to him and you're okay! He was in the wall and you -- you talked to him." Justin frowned. He shivered, but this time not in pleasure. A man in the wall. In the dark. In a hole.

She darted a glance back at the house on the hill then looped her arm through his. She started them walking toward their homes again. "It was like I had to talk to him, Justin. Like I couldn't say no or move away! At the time, I wasn't afraid. But I *should* have been."

They were now outside Ellen's house. The porch light was on and a pumpkin with a candle inside was blazing merrily on the steps. Halloween was the next day. It was Justin's absolute favorite time of year. He couldn't wait for it. This time Ellen was dressing up as Dr. Frankenstein and he was going to be the monster.

I didn't expect that we would be involved in a real supernatural event now! Again, the excitement trumped the fear and any unease he felt. Ellen though truly looked scared and she was never scared.

24

"Let's go in your house. Show me this tunnel," Justin said as he tried to steer them towards her porch.

Maybe he'll be there and I'll get a chance to talk to him no matter what El wants.

"No! Absolutely not!" She pressed her hands against his chest. "He wants me to bring you down there. He wants to talk to you. And that means, he mustn't get those things until and unless we know what he's all about."

Again, he experienced that feeling of soaring electricity at the thought that this being wanted him. His forehead furrowed. "If he got into your house, and you said he has tunnels to every house in Winter Haven, why not just come to mine if he wants to see me so badly?"

"Because the people who were in my house before we moved in did something. Some ritual. It's the only way he can come," she whispered. "Your house is still barred to him. That's what he said."

"Well, the lore says that vampires can't get inside your house unless you invite them," he murmured. He tapped his lower lip with his index finger as he pondered the situation. "Maybe it's something like that."

"Justin!" She hit his side lightly. "You're still not listening to me! I don't want *you* anywhere near him. I don't want him near *me*!"

Justin shook himself to try and focus. "Have you told your folks?"

"I told them about the hole," she said. "But I knew they wouldn't believe me about the man so I kept that back."

Justin could well imagine how Ellen's hyper-intellectual parents would react to their daughter claiming that there was a man in a tunnel behind the wall. She'd be carted off to see a psychiatrist before she even got the words out.

"What did they say?" Justin asked.

"My dad was all upset, but he just said he'd get someone in to fix the wall soon. But I had this strange feeling that he won't.

That he'll *forget* just like I did about it." She rubbed her hands together. "Dad just shoved the bricks back in that the man had pushed out. But the man ... he'll just push them back out again. He was working on the cement of the others while we talked last night. But he didn't want to draw too much attention to it until -- until I brought you over tonight."

Justin's heart beat faster. But Ellen was scared of the man. She didn't want him in her house. "Maybe you should stay at my place tonight then."

"I can't leave my parents alone to face him if he breaks through. I'm the only one between him and them! I have to stay," she answered. Her eyes kept flickering to the doorway of her house like she expected to see something bad there.

"Then maybe I should sneak into your place tonight so you won't be alone," he offered. He told himself he was doing it so that she would be safe and not because he wanted to meet the man from the house. "I won't go down to the basement, but I'll make sure that nothing comes up either. I'll make sure you don't go down, too. Especially since it sounds like he is capable of some sort of *compulsion.*"

"No, Justin. Until my dad has the wall fixed and I can figure out how to *really* close it up to him, you're not coming over. I don't know what the man will do if you come," she whispered.

"What does he want with me?" Justin saw himself as just a gawky eighteen-year-old kid. He was nothing special. More like different and weird than special. But he believed in things that other people didn't. Maybe the man knew that about him.

She stared at him long and hard until he was shifting from foot to foot once more. Finally, she said, "He didn't say."

But Justin knew that she was lying. She didn't lie to him normally so that was disturbing in and of itself. It also pissed him off. "I can't help you if you lie to me, El. Let me help you. Tell me what he said!"

She pressed one hand over his heart. It was a tender gesture and that ancient look in her eyes was back. "You are helping me. Just -- just don't come over, okay? Not until I get this sorted."

"How are you going to get it sorted, El? The Internet isn't going to have an answer for this! You don't even know *what* he is!" Justin's hands flew up in the air.

"There are old boxes of books in the attic from the previous owners. I think there might be an answer in them. After all, they knew what he was and how to invite him in," she explained.

"I don't know," he said. Part of him was anxious about her failing in her research and another part of him was anxious about her succeeding in it.

But even if she keeps him out of her house, I can always go to his. A thrill went through him. He clamped down on the thought. What if El was right to be scared? He should let her do some research before he acted himself.

"I should go in. I want to get started researching. And we've got that calculus quiz tomorrow, remember?" She arched an eyebrow at him.

He was doing badly in math. Justin sighed. "You think I can study calculus after *this*?" She shrugged and her gaze told him that she wasn't going to be studying either. "Promise you'll get online and we'll chat about everything you're finding in your research, okay?"

She nodded and turned to walk into her house. Later he'd wish that he had grabbed her and hugged her. He'd wish that he had insisted she tell her parents about the man. He'd wish that he'd made her stay with him. He'd wish that he had done whatever it took to stop her from going into that house.

The last time he ever saw her was as she was opening the screen door to go in. He had already been on his way home when she'd actually disappeared from view. But he hadn't stayed to watch

27

her go, because he didn't know it would be the last of her he would ever see.

Chapter 3

What Lies Beneath

Dinner was interminable. All Justin could think about was getting up to his room and talking to Ellen online. Then he'd know what was happening with the tunnel and the man. He squirmed in his seat. Thinking of the man made him feel all warm inside. It was ridiculous to be flattered, but then it was ridiculous not to be. Something otherworldly wanted to talk to him!

He's imprisoned. He can only travel through midnight black tunnels. He's likely to be hideous. Probably a monster, Justin firmly told himself, but his mind kept offering a different picture. *His hair will be prematurely white with a silvery sheen. It'll hang down to the middle of his back. He doesn't cut it because why should he? It's not like he cares about the fashion of the day. And there's no one to run his or her hands through it and feel how silky it is. But he imagines a*

29

time when there will be.   He longs for it.   His face will be pale as
marble.   But he'll have startling silver eyes.   He'll wear the slightest
of smiles that will reveal white, sharp teeth ...

Justin jerked at the table.   He hadn't meant to lose himself in his thoughts.   His parents stared at him a moment and then both laughed.

"Caught up in a daydream, were you, Justin?" his father asked.

Justin blushed. If his father had any idea what he daydreamed about, he was sure that he'd be treated to the patented Jack Devereaux frown. He was already a big disappointment to the older man. He wasn't into sports or cars or anything his father could relate to. To find out he was into guys as well might be too much.

"You've been awfully quiet tonight," his mother Marie noted.

"Ellen and I were talking about the house," he said.   His mouth went dry.   He never brought the house up with his parents. He didn't know why.   It just felt private. But he could think of nothing else right at that moment. Perhaps his parents knew something about it.   Maybe there was local lore he hadn't yet heard.

Marie frowned. "The house? Our house? Hers?"

"The LaMascares Mansion," Justin clarified.

Both of his parents froze. Their eyes met over the table and something passed between them that Justin couldn't catch.   Jack took a drink of water then carefully set the glass down. He turned to Justin with a grim expression.

"What were you talking about exactly?" Jack asked.

Justin shifted under his father's piercing gaze. His eyes skittered over to his mother. He was struck again by how he looked nothing like them.   His father was blond and hearty. His mother had light brown hair and laughing brown eyes.   Both of them had golden complexions year round while he was pale as a ghost all the time. His black hair and clear gray eyes didn't come from them.

So where did they come from? The milkman? The postman? When I bring it up, neither of them will say. They laugh and brush it off. But the laughter doesn't reach their eyes.

"We were just talking." Justin shrugged and drew his fork through his mashed potatoes.

His parents had on their "iceberg expressions." He called them that because what was on the surface was so small compared to what they were feeling underneath.

"Tell me that you haven't been hanging around that house," Jack demanded. His golden tan had turned a ruddy color on his cheeks. "You've always been good and stayed away from it. Tell me you haven't --"

"Been good? Wait a sec -- what's the big deal about the house?" Justin asked. But he knew what the big deal was: it was occupied by a man who made tunnels. But his parents couldn't know that. They were prosaic. They didn't believe in monsters.

"It's dangerous. It's falling apart. You need to stay away from there," Marie said firmly. Her hands were clenched in front of her on the tabletop. Her knuckles were white.

"No, it's not!" Justin snapped. "The house is perfectly fine. You can tell just by looking at it that it's not a ruin." His parents both went silent. "So ... what's the real deal here?"

He expected his father to get mad and demand that he apologize for speaking to them like that. Jack had a temper. His blue eyes would flash and he'd slam his fist down on the Formica table top. But he didn't tonight. In fact, he seemed to deflate. He ran a hand through his thick blond hair and leaned back in his seat.

But it was his mother who spoke, "People died in that house, Justin."

"What?" Something cold wound around his heart. "No, I would have found out ..." He snapped his mouth shut. He'd done Internet searches on the house of course, it was his obsession after all. Nothing had ever come up. A murder would have or he thought it would.

"Found out?" Jack's voice was sharp.

Justin sank down into his chair. His father hadn't missed his slip. "It sort of just looms there. It's a cool house. So ... I don't know. I was just curious about it."

His parents stared at him for long moments. Finally, his mother nodded as if satisfied with his explanation. His shoulders sagged in relief.

"It happened when you were a baby," Marie said. Her eyes became unfocused as she remembered.

"Who died, Mom?" Justin asked simply.

"Children," she said. "And then ... everyone who lived in that house."

"There are people and places where evil lives," Jack said suddenly. "I never believed that before. But I did after that night."

"You're sorta freaking me out." Justin crossed his arms over his thin chest.

Evil. There it is again. First El and now my parents!

"We need you to be so you'll stay away from that house and everything to do with it." Jack raised bleak eyes to Justin and reached for Justin's shoulder. He wasn't a touchy-feely man. Justin could count on one hand the number of hugs and pats he'd received from Jack over the years. The boy froze when that work-roughened hand brushed against his neck.

"The LaMascares owned the property for as long as anyone can remember," Marie explained. "They founded the town. They were an ancient aristocratic family that had come from Europe after some ... unpleasantness there."

"Same damned *unpleasantness* they started here," Jack put in. "They were run off. Either be burned in Europe or go to America. Guess we know which one they chose."

"What did they do?" Justin demanded to know.

"Necromancy," Marie whispered.

"Necro--necromancy?" Justin stared at her.

"The year after you were born, children started to disappear from town," Marie said. "I was almost grateful then that we couldn't -- well, that you were a baby and so you were never out of our sight."

Jack reached across and covered his wife's clenched hands. "It was monstrous what they were doing."

"They killed kids?" The words felt exotic on Justin's tongue, unbelievable in a way he couldn't explain.

Marie nodded. "The LaMascares were sacrificing those poor little children in this underground chapel --"

"Underground?" Justin interrupted sharply.

Underground. Tunnels. The man.

"Yes, beneath the whole town of Winter Haven there are caverns connected by countless tunnels. There's even supposed to be a huge river that runs to the sea," Marie said.

"Oh, I -- I didn't know that," Justin said faintly.

El needs to hear this!

His mother, thankfully, was too distracted by what she was saying to notice the strangeness of his reactions to her statements. She continued on, "The LaMascares stretched the children's little bodies over this altar and -- and just ended them."

Justin felt cold. Icy. "What does killing kids have to do with necromancy?"

What did *anything* have to do with necromancy?

"They believed it would bring back the progenitor of their line: Peren LaMascares. They claimed they needed the energy of young life to bring him back across the Veil," Marie explained.

"You're kidding! I -- I guess anyone who believes in necromancy has to be a little off," Justin's voice faded as his parent's serious expressions. "The LaMascares didn't succeed in bringing him back though, right?" He tried to make it sound joking,

33

but all he could think about was the man in the wall, talking to Ellen in the dark, wanting to know about him.

"No. They were stopped," Marie said.

"You act like they could have done it though." Justin's gaze jumped from one parent to the other. Neither answered him. He ran a hand through his short hair. "Why did they want him back?"

"The LaMascares claimed that his powers would allow them to bring back the old gods that lay sleeping in drowned cities," Marie paused. "They made this future sound almost wonderful until you remembered it was drenched in children's blood."

Justin could almost see those cities for a moment: eldritch towers reaching up from the deepest fathoms, alien architecture that would make a human mind spin with their beauty and terror, and within these cities, in night-guarded tombs, would lay the undying, forgotten gods, waiting only for the stars to be in the right alignment and the correct words to be spoken. He shook himself. The imagery alone had almost cast a spell over him. Yet it couldn't be real.

"How do you know all this?" Justin asked. "Did you know the LaMascares?"

His parents exchanged uneasy glances. His mother's eyes then went down to her hands.

"Everyone knew," Jack said hollowly.

But that didn't sound right to Justin. Surely the LaMascares weren't blasting their plans for child-killing, necromancy and world domination to everyone in town. But at the same time, he couldn't see his own parents as being the sort that the LaMascares would befriend and vice versa. "Okay, so they were killing kids to bring back some long dead guy, but clearly it didn't work and there aren't any LaMascares in town any more, right?"

"All the LaMascares are dead," Marie said. This time she looked at him, unblinking, as if to push the words into him. "Dead and gone. But the house ..."

"There are still ways down to the underground through it. It isn't safe," Jack cut in. "That's why we don't want you anywhere near it. I know with Halloween coming up kids do stupid things, but the LaMascares Mansion is off limits."

"We were just talking about it. Not planning on going inside," Justin assured them. But that was the joke, wasn't it? His parents were worried about him going to the house when the house was coming to him, was looking for him. "I've never heard about any of this. Not in town. Not on the Internet. Not anywhere. How could something this big not be reported? I mean dead kids? Necromancy?"

"It was reported locally, but then there was an agreement that it wouldn't be discussed any longer. Everyone thought that was best," Marie explained. "So all the records of it happening were expunged."

"You know Winter Haven, son. We don't like outsiders in our business," Jack said as if that was explanation enough for hiding the murder of children.

The man told Ellen that he was imprisoned in the house. My parents are saying that all of the LaMascares were killed that night in the house nearly twenty years ago, which is the same time period as he has been trapped inside. Could he be Peren LaMascares? Was he half brought back by the LaMascares' sacrifices, but not all the way? But why would he want to talk to me? What do I matter to him?

Justin rose from his seat on slightly unsteady legs. "Well, I have a lot of homework to do. Calculus test tomorrow. I'm going to head up."

He had to talk to Ellen about this. He had to warn her. Talking to the man in the basement was completely off limits for both of them.

"So you won't go to the LaMascares Mansion?" Marie asked.

Justin gave her an honest smile. "No, of course not. Totally get it. Won't go near the place."

Because he didn't need to. The LaMascares were coming here.

"That's good, son. We're glad you understand." Jack gave him a relieved smile.

Justin nodded and slowly backed away from the dinner table. He turned and nearly fled to his room. He was afraid they might guess he was lying if he stayed a moment more.

CHAPTER 4

SEEING THINGS

*J*ustin raced up the stairs to his bedroom. He shut the door behind him and rested his back against it. His chest felt tight and he couldn't get enough air. He clutched the front of his hoodie and concentrated on breathing. In and out. In and out. Finally, the anxiety cooled and his chest fully expanded again. The vise-like feeling then left. His shoulders slumped and he brushed his hand through his hair.

Necromancers. Dead kids. Peren LaMascares. It was all madness.

He pushed himself off the door and fished inside his pocket for his cell phone to call Ellen, but froze in mid-step. His gaze went to the window. He could see the LaMascares Mansion. The last rays of sun limned its outline. He twitched as he imagined a pale creature staring back at him from the uppermost windows. Or was Peren already in the night-haunted tunnels making his way to Ellen's house? He jerked the shade down and sat at his desk.

He picked Ellen's name from his phone's contacts and pressed the call button, but her cell just rang a few times and then went to voicemail. He told himself that she was just eating dinner. Her parents had a strict no-phones rule at the dinner table. He left a message for her to call him back ASAP and also sent her a text with the same request. He should just go to her house and he would. But he wanted to just check one thing.

His moved the mouse to his computer and the screensaver of an unending sky disappeared. He got online. He typed LaMascares as a search term and hit enter. He had done this countless times and had found nothing. But, for some reason, he thought it would be different this time. There was nothing about the murders in Winter Haven. The city's ability to hide from the world what it didn't want known was on full display, but there was one link that he had never seen before. One lone, solitary link. He clicked it. It lead to a blog with only one entry in it. It was date about a year ago, which made it strange that it had never come up before in all his searches. Black background. Green text. He read the entry.

I wanted to know who I was. Now I wish I had never found out. This will be my last entry and I wonder if it will be deleted, too, like I will be. Deleted. Wiped away. Gone. I'll be replaced and no one will know. Not even me.

I am a LaMascares. I wish I was the last. But I know that there are others. And so does he. He's one of us. The first of us. In the beginning, I tried to locate my family. I thought I could at least warn the others. But now I know my efforts would just lead him to them all that much faster. He'll find them eventually, but I won't give him directions. I'll give those unknown brothers, sisters, cousins, nephews and nieces I have out there a chance to have an hour, a day, a week, a month, a year more of blessed ignorance.

Even now when I know I must end myself to stop being overwritten by my LaMascares' self, I hesitate. I love life. I want to live. But not as a LaMascares ....

38

Only why shouldn't I live as one? We have a long and glorious lineage stretching back before written history. We have survived in the dark, waiting until that fateful day we can raise the gods that are ours, to have the humans bow before us as they should. We are the elite! Forged in fires hotter than Hell. We came out like bright, sharp blades ready to cut down those that stand in our way! We are born rulers. The rest are cattle.

No, I won't kill myself! I won't surrender to this pathetic clutching of the pedestrian life! I will embrace my birthright and --

I look back at what I just wrote and I don't remember doing it. All my other posts are deleted. I did this ... no, HE did. The LaMascares inside me did this. I have to end myself before he does.

Now.

There was nothing else. No indication who had written this. It was dated about a year ago. Had they killed themselves? Were they mad? They had to be crazy, of course. Or maybe it was some sort of joke. A piece of modern art thrown up on the web. There were no answers there other than ones that Justin didn't want to contemplate.

He looked at his phone. Ellen hadn't called back. Hadn't texted either. He grabbed the phone and rose from his desk chair. He dialed her number as he took the stairs two at a time down to the first floor. Again, his call went to voicemail right away. He left another shaky message as he pushed through the front door, moving carefully so that it didn't squeak and alert his parents that he was going out.

But he had not been careful enough. His mom called after him, asking where he was going, but his throat was too tight with fear to answer her. Nothing could have happened to Ellen. She had to be safe. People like Ellen, special and unique and precious and his best friend, didn't die by the hands of monsters. They lived life, went to MIT, made impossibly important discoveries and were feted

39

as the greatest scientist of their generation. Two unanswered phone calls did not mean that was all wiped away.

Deleted.

The fifty feet between his front door and Ellen's suddenly seemed miles away. His legs wouldn't go as fast as he wanted them to. It was like he was running through molasses. The wind picked up and one particularly icy blast seemed intent on keeping him from reaching her house. He stretched his arms out, grabbed one of the pillars on the porch and pulled himself up the front steps. As soon as he set foot on the porch, the wind subsided, almost as if it had never been.

Was that real? Is any of this real?

He smoothed his hands over the front of his shirt. They shook. He wrenched open the screen door to Ellen's house and prepared to pound on the main door until someone unlocked it. But he noticed that the main door was slightly ajar. He pushed it open and stepped inside the preternaturally quiet house. The scent of roast beef and honey-glazed carrots rolled over him, but there was another scent underneath these homey smells. Something sweet and rotten.

His eyes strayed toward the doorway to the kitchen. There was a roast out on a white serving dish on the counter as if Ellen's mother was preparing to wrap it up and place it in the refrigerator for the next day's leftovers. The door of the dishwasher was open. He saw that it had been half emptied. A pile of gleaming plates sat beside the sink. Ellen's father had evidently stopped mid-task as well. Both parents had abruptly ended what they were doing. The question was why?

Justin walked down the hallway toward the basement stairs at the back of the house. He winced each time he stepped on a loose board and the floor creaked.

Why am I trying to be quiet? Don't I want Ellen and her parents to know I'm here? What if they're hurt? They could call out if they knew someone was here to help them.

But he didn't believe that. He sensed there was no one living in the house. It felt empty. Like the famous ship the Marie Celeste. The ship was discovered empty, food on plates that had never been eaten or cleared, no sign of emergency, but no crew either. Justin thought of the unwrapped roast and swallowed hard.

He stepped in front of the open door to the basement. The lights were on and that almost made it worse. If it was dark down there, he would have had an excuse not to go down, to go back to his own house to grab a flashlight. But since the lights were on he had to keep going. His heart stuttered in his chest and a bad metallic taste flooded his mouth. It was inconceivable that Ellen should be gone so if he acted like this was a normal night where there was no chance for her to be gone -- *deleted* -- then maybe reality would shift to meet his wish.

I should call out to her. Tell her I'm here. I don't want to startle her.

But he kept his lips firmly pressed together as he crept down the basement stairs. It was one flight that ended in a carpeted area. This front part of the basement had been finished. The cold stone floor was covered in beige carpeting, the walls were affixed with drywall, and there was a cozy seating area and a surround-sound theater system. It was Ellen's father's man-cave. That he only watched the Discovery channel down there wasn't the point. He had a space where he could by himself. He often let Ellen and Justin have it though, because he would rather spend his time reading on the porch or in the sun room. Justin felt a sweeping sense of loss flow over him.

They aren't dead. They can't be. Snap out of it!

Justin turned his head toward the seating area to see if Ellen's father was parked there with a book. Maybe the whole family was with him. But the silence told him that wasn't true even before his eyes confirmed it. He stepped softly toward the adjoining room, or the middle basement where the washer and dryer were kept. The

41

floor in there was raw concrete. The earthy, cold tang of stone and water hit his nose. It was colder in this middle section. The lights were on in there, too. The washer and dryer just sat there like white sentinels of domesticity. But no one was using them. Ellen's mother didn't stand up from pulling clothes out of the dryer and tell him cheerily that Ellen was up in her room studying for tomorrow's calculus exam -- and shouldn't he be doing the same? -- she might ask with a small smile.

That left only the back basement to search. It contained old furniture, stacks of moldering magazines, and toys that Ellen no longer had an interest in. When they were younger, he and Ellen had played down in the back basement. They pretended that they were archeologists in search of ancient treasure. Seeing the bare concrete walls and broken furniture now made him wonder why they had ever found it inviting to play down there.

It feels claustrophobic. And the shadows are all wrong. They are too many of them where there shouldn't be. I remember feeling safe down here back then. But not now.

His eyes scanned the walls for the bricked up spot that Ellen had talked about. He didn't see anything. But then it hit him. He knew where it had to be. There was a little room attached to the main part of the back basement. That was the only room that wasn't lit up. But the light from the back basement spilled halfway into it.

I'm breaking all the rules, too, El. Hopefully, we'll get a chance to laugh about it later.

With his heart in his throat, Justin crept slowly forward. He looked feverishly for signs of Ellen and her parents. He didn't see anything at first but bare floor and walls bathed in shadows. Then he caught sight of a book lying open on the ground. It was an old book. It had a leather cover and the spine was cracked with age. A musty odor rose off it as he picked it up and turned it over. There were elaborate symbols drawn all along the margins. But in the center panel, written in a spidery hand, was a spell that allegedly closed the gates to the undead. When Justin looked at the words, his eyes itched and burned. He blinked rapidly and after the feeling subsided, he looked down at that page again. It had changed. The words were not as he had first read them -- and, he guessed, as Ellen had understood them.

It isn't a spell to keep the undead out. It's one to let them in. Oh, my God, no ... This -- this is -- no, it's just not possible! Did Ellen let Peren in when she thought she was keeping him out?

Ellen had tried this spell. He knew it. He could almost hear her lecturing him that there was no magic. Magic was just science we hadn't discovered yet. But where was she? Had Peren taken her?

His gaze had swept up to the wall where the tunnel had been. "Had" was the operative word. The stone bricks that the workmen used to patch up the wall were scattered into the room as if someone had burst through them from the tunnel side. But the tunnel itself was gone. Perhaps it had collapsed as Ellen had finished the incantation. Dirt, roots and rocks were sifting into the basement floor from where the tunnel had been. But there was one more thing that he saw. Sticking out of the dirt from the center of what used to be the opening, as if motioning him inside, was a single human hand.

BIRTH RITE

CHAPTER 5

THE WORM

*J*ustin let out a cry of horror as the outstretched hand suddenly began to retract into the dirt. Then he realized the hand wasn't moving on its own. The dirt, stones and roots that had spilled into the basement were also moving as something -- *some creature* -- closed its jaws.

It's a worm! A gigantic white worm with tusk-sized teeth!

Justin stepped backwards and slipped. He fell hard onto his ass. He scuttled further away until his back slammed against the wall. The worm's mouth was circular. It was as wide and tall as the opening into the basement itself, which was six feet by six feet. Its brownish-white teeth were the size of rhino horns and they lined every inch of its circular mouth. Its skin was an unwholesome white. It gave off a slight glow like phosphorescent mold. The smell that he had caught wind of upstairs suddenly became overwhelming. The sweetness of rot and the raw scent of sewage hit Justin like a brick wall. He clutched at his throat and gagged. The worm swallowed fully then. The debris and the body disappeared inside of it.

Who was it? Ellen? Her mother? Her father? I didn't see! I couldn't tell!

The shock that his best friend and her parents were probably now inside the belly of the monster that weaved blindly in front of him held Justin frozen in place. He hardly felt the tears streaming down his cheeks. He felt responsible for their deaths though he didn't know why. He thought of Ellen's description of the tunnels: *circular and perfect.* He guessed now that the worm had made the tunnels for Peren.

Does he send the worm out to all the houses? Or just the ones he wants to get into?

Impotent rage suffused with grief and fear filled him. His elfin features darkened with it. His friend was dead. Her parents were dead. And soon, he would be, too, unless he got out of there. Faced with the horror of the worm, he could only imagine what else Peren was capable of. What did the LaMascares' progenitor want with Ellen and him?

The worm's head swayed from side to side as if looking for him. It couldn't actually see him as it was eyeless. It had no need to see underground. No need for ears either. He guessed that it acted by touch and felt vibrations from movement. Justin imagined the creature slithering its way through night-filled caverns for eons with only the soft glow of its body to illuminate its path. He could envision the mighty stalactites and stalagmites that lined the ancient roads it wandered. Then his mind offered up an image of carved stone beyond the beast in his vision. A pale temple amidst the natural gloom.

One of the tombs of the old gods, a voice whispered to him. *We will waken them and they will stride forth onto the lands above. Taking back what is ours.*

46

Justin blinked the strange imagery away. Now was not the time to be daydreaming! But it hadn't felt like a dream. More like a nightmare ... but *real*. When the worm's head turned away from him, Justin slowly inched his way toward the door out of the small back room. The worm's head stopped moving. Justin held his breath. Finally, the worm began to sway again. Justin crab-walked at a snail's pace away from it. One arm stretched behind him then the other. One foot supporting him then the other. His shoes crunched in the grit on the floor. The noise wasn't loud but to Justin it sounded like a gunshot. The worm stilled.

Its bulk suddenly reared back, mouth opening wide, teeth dripping steaming saliva onto the floor in large puddles. The hot stink from its open maw caused him to gasp. The worm shuddered and arched its back as if to let fly a triumphant howl. Justin scrambled to his feet and blindly ran. He heard the worm slam onto the floor where he had been. The blow shook the house and his feet flew out from under him, his knees smashing against an old dresser. Pain streaked up through his legs. Justin let out a shrill cry before forcing himself up again. The worm was surely right behind him. Its fetid stink surrounded him.

He bounded up the basement stairs and flew into the hallway. He let out a low moan of gratefulness as he saw the open front door. He was about to rush out when the whole house shook. He hadn't thought about the fact that a creature that could tunnel through stone would have no problem with a wooden floor. There was a cracking sound as the wooden boards of the floor snapped and the worm burst up from the basement. Half its bulk landed thunderously on what was left of the hallway. Justin flew backward. Stunned, he slid to the ground. Blood trickled down from his temple. The worm let out a roar and adrenaline squirted into Justin's bloodstream.

Ignoring the pain, he tried to move his right hand to hoist himself up. But it was hooked on something. He twisted his head to the side to see what it was. The door handle! He was lying against the back door. He wrenched the door open and slid out onto the back steps. He felt the house shudder behind him. There were snaps and screams as wood and metal were wrenched in unnatural ways. He used his elbows to drag himself down the steps and into the back yard. Blood streamed his face from myriad of cuts on his forehead and scalp. His body ached in places he had never thought about. But he didn't care, he just needed to get out.

The sound of the house collapsing behind him was deafening. The air buffeted all around him as the two story colonial pancaked. Dust flooded the air and he couldn't see anything. He just kept crawling forward. He feared the worm would squirm out of the rubble and hurl its bulk toward him at any moment. The thought of being crushed under its gelatinous body or enveloped by its teeth-encrusted mouth was terrifying. But his strength drained from him as his lungs filled with dust. He curled up and coughed until his throat ached.

"Mom! Dad!" he called out. Surely they had heard the destruction of Ellen's home. They were undoubtedly outside looking for him. He wanted them so badly. Needed them.

Ellen's dead! Her parents are dead! The worm! Oh, my God, the worm!

He began to sob. He couldn't imagine a world with the worm, but without Ellen. She had so much to offer. She was going to change the world with that intellect of hers. She would have. But now she was gone. And Ellen didn't believe in an afterlife or reincarnation. She thought that this life was all there was. Oddly, her death had proved to him that there was clearly something more. Only he wasn't sure if it was a good something. Perhaps the nighted caverns he had glimpsed for a moment were where the souls of the dead went. Perhaps Ellen walked there now, trying to help others, in the endless blackness. He shuddered. Such a terrible fate. So very wrong for his beloved best friend.

48

If I had the LaMascares' power I would bring Ellen back to life. I wouldn't be some foul necromancer bastard that sets worms on people!

But he did not truly think that he could ever do such a thing. To wield the power of life and death. To bring back one who was worthy of life in exchange for one worthy of death. He was sure that such a power could never be his to command. Justin suddenly froze at the sound of footsteps walking toward him. He blinked rapidly, but the dust was still thick and blood dripped into his eyes.

"Mom? Dad?" he called out hopefully.

It wasn't the worm heading toward him. The sounds were too soft. Subtle. It was definitely a person. He could hear the crunch of leaves underfoot. He raised his head and narrowed his eyes, peering into the gloom. A single figure approached him. He blinked and stared harder. The person was as tall as his father, perhaps not as broad though strongly built. It was a man despite the fact that he had long platinum hair that hung down to the middle of his chest. He was more than just handsome. He had a cold, classical beauty that reminded Justin of a Greek statue of a forgotten god.

"Your parents are dead, child," the man said in a voice that sounded as warm as honey on a hot day.

"What?" Grief clogged his throat. The thought of Jack and Marie being dead, too, was like a hit to his solar plexus.

"They were killed by the people of this town in their ignorance soon after you were born," the man explained as he dropped down on his haunches beside Justin.

Justin's brow furrowed. He wasn't talking about Jack and Marie. "You're talking about the LaMascares."

"Yes, I am," the man said with that quiet smile on his lips.

In the beginning, I tried to locate my family, he remembered the unnamed author of the blog had written.

"You've got the wrong guy," Justin said firmly. A trill of unease wormed down his spine.

I thought I could at least warn the others. But now I know my efforts would just lead him to them all that much faster, the writer had said.

There were others. Other LaMascares that lived in ignorance of what and who they were. *Am I one of them?*

"I've been looking for you for so long. But I never thought to glance right under my nose. Here you've been. Less than a mile away and I missed you entirely even as I found others in far flung places." The man laughed softly as if amused at his failure to find Justin sooner.

He'll find them eventually, but I won't give him directions, the writer had claimed.

But he found me. He found me all the same.

"I don't know what you're talking about." Justin pushed himself up to his knees. He gazed over his shoulder at the ruined house. Was the worm coming?

"I think you do." Quiet confidence rang out in the man's voice.

I'll give those unknown brothers, sisters, cousins, nephews and nieces I have out there a chance to have an hour, a day, a week, a month, a year more of blessed ignorance, the writer's words unfurled in Justin's mind.

Why couldn't I have stayed ignorant? Why? Why?

"I -- I n--need to go," Justin stammered out. "There's a -- a thing in the house there. It could come out and --"

"The Thyrumin will not hurt you now. I was very cross with it for frightening you as it has," the man said.

"Thyrumin -- the worm?" Justin gasped. "Who are you?"

"You already know that, too," the man answered.

"You -- you're Peren LaMascares!" Justin exclaimed. He tried to draw away from the man, but his body was as weak as a kitten's.

50

Peren grasped his arm with one long-fingered hand. It felt like a steel shackle. The older man cocked his head to the side. "And you are James LaMascares."

"No. You're wrong. My name is Justin Devereaux," Justin said.

Peren shook his head. "Your parents gave you your name on the Altar of Ashtareth. I heard their prayers for your entry into the Book of Life. Your name is James LaMascares."

"No!" Justin spat.

"Yes. And those people." Peren thrust one hand towards Justin's house. "They came and stole you from your crib after they foully murdered your parents."

"That's crazy!"

"Your mother screamed as Jack Devereaux slit her throat. She was reaching for you, James. She was trying to get to you as Marie picked up your struggling form from your crib," Peren said

Justin shook his head in denial even as he pictured what Peren was telling him. Images of a woman with black hair and gray eyes just like his, reaching out a pale arm to him, while Jack stood behind her, a knife in his upraised arm. He saw another figure. A man covered in blood, still trying to drag himself to a child's crib, even as his guts trailed out of him like obscene ribbons. His father. That was his father. Not Jack.

"The whole of the LaMascares' family was gathered for the ceremony to bring me back. Mothers and fathers. Daughters and sons. So many children. All with our blessed blood running through their veins. Those children watched as their parents were slaughtered. Their young minds scarred by it," Peren uttered.

"I don't -- you're wrong!" But there was no heat in Justin's voice. He didn't believe his own words.

Peren gripped Justin's shoulders. "It was a celebration! But Marie, Jack and more of their ilk rampaged through your home and killed every adult in it. Then they stole the children. Took them for their own. Some moved far away. But some --"

"No, you're lying!"

"Some stayed close by," Peren continued on as if Justin hadn't said anything.

Justin was shaking. His whole body felt alien to him at that moment, like he was a stranger in it. "That can't be true. The LaMascares are murderers! And you -- you're a murderer! A filthy necromancer!"

The man's classically handsome face flushed. Anger danced in his silvery eyes. "You repeat the words of the *vermin*! Under normal circumstances I would punish you for such a transgression! But you are confused and injured." His expression softened. A smile crossed the full pale lips. "You must be re-educated. I see that now. You truly do not understand your heritage nor your place in the world."

"You killed my best friend!" Justin shrieked. "You killed her!"

Peren shook his head. More of his platinum hair spilled over his shoulders as he did so. "Ashtareth demands sacrifice. The Thyrumin would have taken her mother only, but your friend jumped before her. A brave act. But it was fruitless. Both were taken. Then the father struck a blow and he, too, came to know the belly of the Thyrumin."

"You sent that horrible thing to their house!" Justin cried, swiping at the tears on his face.

"It came because of her utterance of the spell in the book. Those who lived in her home before her set the course upon which she tread. Not I," Peren said.

"I -- I don't believe that. Those people did what they did for *you*!" Justin argued weakly. His head was swimming with pain.

"They did it for the greater glory. We are gods among men, James. You will understand," Peren said.

"I'll never understand. I'll never be like you or the other LaMascares!"

But Peren did not look impressed. "You are injured. You must rest. Your utterances reflect your state of mind."

Justin's mouth opened in shock. He felt like a little child that had just been told to stop bawling his eyes out and take his medicine. Anger flared inside of him, but it soon turned to surprise as Peren lifted him up easily in his arms.

"What are you doing?" Justin squawked.

The solid chest against his side felt strange. He had never been held by a man before. Peren's silky hair tickled his cheek. Justin struggled against the strong arms that held him fast. He expected Peren to smell of the grave. The older man was brought back from the dead after all. Yet Peren's scent was that of cinnamon and clove. His body felt firm and well-muscled. There was none of the softness of decay. There was nothing of the corpse about him whatsoever.

"Hush, child. Stop your squirming. You are inflaming my loins and you are not in any state for such games at the moment," Peren chided gently.

"Inflaming your what?" Justin cried.

Peren threw his head back with a laugh. "Do not claim innocence. I can tell you yearn for the body of another man to lay with you. Your thoughts show me this." The silvery eyes narrowed at him and Justin felt like the other man was looking into his soul. "In fact, you have yearned for *me* to lay with you. We will see if you deserve such a reward later."

Justin's mouth opened to protest. But Peren's gaze locked with his and his will to object crumbled. He slumped against Peren's chest. His eyes fluttered half-shut within moments. The pull of sleep was overwhelming. He thought he heard Marie and Jack calling his name, but their voices sounded like they were coming from far away and were smothered by hundreds of feet of soil and stone.

"They'll come for me. My mom and dad will come to rescue me," Justin murmured against Peren's throat.

He heard the smile in the older man's voice as Peren said, "I am counting on that."

CHAPTER 6

SURRENDER

*J*ustin awoke slowly. His first impression was of softness surrounding him. Silk underneath his cheek and a feathery mattress beneath his bare back, buttocks and legs. He shivered as he felt the warmth of the blanket on top of him was carefully pulled back from his naked form. A wet towel ran along his stomach then trailed down to his crotch. He moaned softly as his thighs were parted and the towel smoothed between then. His hips lifted helplessly as arousal coursed through his young body.

"So responsive," Peren murmured with approval as he stroked Justin's cock with the cloth.

The boy mewled and his cock hardened and lengthened under Peren's ministrations. His eyes opened to slits. The room was lit only with candlelight. He guessed that it was a bedroom in the LaMascares Mansion. He was lying on a four-poster antique bed under silken bedding. Peren sat beside him, wearing only a pair of crimson silk pajama pants. His bare chest was highly muscled and, again, reminded Justin of an ancient Greek statue he had seen in the local museum.

Inhumanly perfect. How can someone so evil be so beautiful?

Peren's face was lovelier than he had ever imagined it. The lines were classical, aristocratic, but with a softening of that marble hardness. Those silvery eyes bore into his soul. Justin was lost on a sea of sensation as the older man discarded the cloth and cupped Justin's erection with one bare hand. The boy arched up with a gasp.

"What are you doing? No -- no -- oooooooohhhhhhh, please," Justin cried out, unsure at the end if he was begging Peren to stop or keep going.

Peren's thumb parted the slit of his cock and precum bubbled out. "Your sweet cock begs to differ with you."

The head of Justin's cock flushed a darker rose, while the shaft had a pinkish hue. His penis curled up toward his stomach.

"Have you ever been touched?" Peren asked.

"None of your business! Get your hands off of me!" Justin managed to grit out. His body was on fire. All it wanted was to be touched more and Peren was so skilled at doing that touching. But he was no one's plaything!

Peren fingered his balls and the boy's legs spread wider as if to give him further access. Shame caused Justin to blush hotly, but he felt unable to resist the older man. Peren smiled even as he lightly slapped Justin's thigh in punishment. His skin stung where he was struck.

"Ow!" Justin complained, rubbing the injured flesh.

Peren feathered his hand in Justin's hair. "Let that be a lesson to you. I am not one to be trifled with or lied to. Your body is telling me quite clearly that it wants my touch. Your mouth shall not deny it."

Justin swallowed. "My body doesn't know any better, but my head does. I don't ..." The boy bit back the words. "I may want you but it's wrong. This is wrong. All of it!"

56

Peren clucked lightly. "Do you always fight so hard against what you want? Are your true desires so frightening to you that you must deny them?"

"Desire is fine! It's great! But not for *you!* What you did to Ellen --"

Peren placed a firm finger over his lips to silence him. "I explained that. Your pain is understandable. And it is instructive."

"Instructive?" Justin burst out.

"Indeed. For it is such a pain that caused me to delve deep into the art of necromancy. The love I felt for my beloved dead children caused me to seek out the powers of darkness," he said.

Justin frowned. He felt a stirring of unwanted empathy for the other man. "Did they die of a disease or something?"

Peren trailed his fingers alone Justin's inner thigh as he answered, "They were brutally murdered by the Church. They claimed I was a worshipper of Satan, but I was not."

"Not then," Justin said.

"I became what they called me in revenge!" Peren's eyes flashed. "And it was not from the Church's weak version of evil that I sought help, but from beings older than this world! They heard my call. My children were brought back to me then. And they shall be returned from the vast gulfs once more!"

Justin's breath caught as a wild thought filled his mind. "Can you bring back Ellen? Can – can you undo all this?"

Peren's gaze became speculative. "I would be willing to do so under certain conditions."

"What conditions?" Justin was incredibly aware of the man's hand on his thigh, how his fingers brushed tantalizingly close to Justin's balls.

Peren laughed darkly, reading Justin's thoughts easily. "Not in exchange for sex, beautiful boy. You will give that to me freely and with great pleasure. I shall take you again and again. No, what I want from you is something much harder for you to give."

"What? I'll -- I'll do it whatever it is!" Justin said. He winced as he heard the desperation in his voice. Ellen's frowning face flashed before his mind's eye. He knew she wouldn't approve of what he was going to do, but he was going to do it anyways.

Because if I don't do this, I'll never see that frown again. She can't be disappointed with me unless she's brought back. And then she can have the life she was meant to live. She can help people! On average it will work out. Peren's evil balanced by her good.

Peren lowered his head so that their lips were but an inch apart. The older man's breath puffed warmly against his mouth. "You must become a LaMascares. Be the man you were born to be. Forget this Justin Devereaux and be James LaMascares."

Justin stared up into the silvery, inhuman eyes and swallowed hard. "If I say yes, will you promise to bring Ellen and her family back?"

Peren's eyes glittered. "I promise it."

Justin's mouth was as dry as dust. He believed Peren. What the older man was asking wasn't that bad, was it? It was just a name change. It meant nothing. He could say whatever Peren wanted. What did it matter if he got Ellen back? So he'd play along. He'd be James LaMascares on the outside, but on the inside he would still be Justin Devereaux. Ellen and her family would be alive. That was the best bargain he could ever hope to get.

"Then -- then, yes, I will be James LaMascares."

Justin swore at that moment he felt the string that connected him to his old life suddenly snap. He let out a soft cry as his very soul seemed adrift in icy currents. For a moment the walls of the bedroom were ripped away and he could once again see those nighted tombs in caverns that rested impossible measures below. Was the door to one of them cracking open? Was something spindly and skeletal slipping toward him? Justin raised his hands up in horror to hold the thing off. But rather than the skeleton's hand he expected to touch him, Peren's warm hand grasped him instead.

"I have you, James. You are safe. I have you. See?" Peren's arms were around him, rocking him against that muscled chest.

Justin sobbed. He clutched at the other man for long moments until the remnants of the vision passed. "What -- what happened?"

"You saw the tomb of Ashtareth. You are blessed. It came out to greet you itself," Peren murmured into his hair.

What have I done? Oh, God, what have I done? But Justin knew that whatever it was, it was done, it was sealed. He could not turn back now.

Justin buried his head between Peren's shoulder and throat. Holding onto the older man was preferable to going back to those haunted caverns in his mind. He curled tighter against Peren. The older man's hands slid up and down his back as he rocked Justin into calmness again.

"I wish to take pleasure in your body, James. Would you find that agreeable?" Peren asked.

The denial died on Justin's lips. He didn't want to lay there and think. He imagined what it would be like to lose himself in sex with this man. To just feel and indulge and give of himself without thought. "Yes, yes I would like that."

Peren smiled. His lips pressed softly at first against Justin's. His tongue flickered along Justin's mouth. The boy parted his lips to let the other man inside. Peren tasted of mint and moss. Justin found himself sucking eagerly on the older man's tongue. He twisted around in Peren's arms so he could plaster his naked form against Peren's semi-clothed one. The older man chuckled into their kiss and helped the boy straddle him.

Justin felt the hard press of Peren's erection between his legs. Peren growled in approval when Justin ground down upon it. He held Justin in place with one hand while he reached for something with the other. Justin eagerly wrapped his arms and legs around Peren, trying to forget all that had happened that night and instead just relishing the hard body of a beautiful man against his own. When he felt Peren part his butt cheeks and play along his crack with his fingers, he moaned appreciatively.

"This will help prepare you for my cock, James. I like to indulge in quite thorough fucking," Peren explained as he pushed something cool and slick against Justin's entrance.

Justin gasped and moaned as something hard and long was gently slid up inside of him. Peren pulled it out, twisted it, and sank it deeper in.

"Oh, God, what -- what is that?" Justin gasped as he clawed at Peren's back.

"A dildo made of Orinthes' horn," he said as the horn rubbed over his prostate.

Justin nearly levitated off the other man. Peren kept a firm hold on his hips, controlling his movements, as he continued to fuck him with the horn. Justin's body trembled as a completely new sensations coursed through him.

"You are a virgin," Peren remarked. He nipped and bit along Justin's jawline.

The boy saw no need to deny it. "Yes, yes --ah, oh, harder, deeper!"

Peren chuckled. "You are clearly made for this."

He thrust the horn in so deep that only a half an inch remained outside of Justin's body. The boy writhed on top of him. He rubbed his penis frantically against Peren's washboard abs. He needed the friction as his insides felt on fire. Peren kissed him deeply and made a low growl.

"You will not have your completion until I am within you," Peren ordered.

Justin was suddenly thrust back onto the bed. Peren spread Justin's legs wide then reached and withdrew the horn. Justin shook as it was removed. His thighs trembled.

"I need -- need to be filled!" he cried out, thrashing his head against the pillows.

"You will be," Peren promised.

Peren slipped off his crimson pants. Justin's breath caught as he saw Peren's cock for the first time. It was large. Much larger than the horn. His hips shifted needily. He bet it would hurt going in, but he would think of nothing else but that large shaft spreading him open. The pain of sex would replace the pain of loss. He licked his lips.

"Take me, Peren. Please, please," Justin begged.

His words seemed to inflame the older man. Peren slicked his cock with something from a sweet-smelling jar at the bedside. His glistening cock pointed toward Justin as if it was a lance and the boy was a target. Justin trembled wildly. Peren lifted the boy's legs above his shoulders, positioning his proud cock against Justin's virgin hole. The pain was incredible as Peren pushed inside. But once the head of his cock popped through Justin's anus, it was as if his body stopped fighting the intrusion.

"Hurts," he groaned.

Peren rubbed gentle circles on his belly. "The pain will pass and the pleasure will remain. Though you are so tight. Oh, gods, you are like a vise on my cock. So good."

Justin surprised himself by trying to push his body farther onto Peren's cock. The older man was holding back.

"I am trying to let your sweet ass adjust, James. I do not want to tear you," Peren explained, gripping Justin's hips hard.

Justin begged with his eyes as he said, "I need you all the way in me."

"I shall be," Peren promised.

He sank in another inch. Justin's mouth parted in a silent cry of pained pleasure as it felt like his ass was being split open and yet the sensation of being filled and connected overrode any agony. Peren began to move his hips slowly. He thrust in slightly then drew out. With each inward push, he delved deeper inside Justin's pliant body. There was a place in Justin that needed to be touched by the necromancer's penis. It throbbed inside of him. He knew that once Peren was all the way in that this place would be satisfied. He was but an inch away from that satisfaction.

"In me, in me, oh, God, in me, please!" Justin nearly screamed.

"All the way in, James, just like you want."

Peren's balls now rested against Justin's buttocks and the place inside of him that needed to be filled burned hotly. The head of the older man's cock rested perfectly in that space. Justin gave out a low mewl. Peren gripped Justin's thighs for a moment, keeping him from moving.

"I'm going to fuck you hard now, James," Peren said.

"Do it. Ah -- do whatever you want!"

Peren pushed Justin's legs tight against the boy's chest. He then began to fuck him. It was like nothing Justin had ever experienced. There was the burn of the huge cock pulling out then slamming back inside. His prostate sizzled as the cock ran along it.

He's going to cum inside of me. Oh, it'll be so good. Feel so perfect, Justin thought as he tipped his hips backward so that Peren could delve as deep as he wanted.

The pace sped up and then slowed down depending on Justin's arousal. It was like Peren was playing his body like an instrument. He brought Justin up to the point of release, until his balls were tight and heavy against his body, his cock dripping like a leaky faucet on his stomach, and then Peren would slow down again and the pleasure went from a volcanic burn to a steady simmer.

"Peren! Please!" Justin begged.

Peren grinned wolfishly down on him. He leaned in and devoured Justin's mouth. Their tongues tangled and Justin sucked eagerly on the other man's lower lip. He wanted more of him, needed more of him. Peren obliged and kissed him until his body ached for lack of oxygen.

"I'm going to cum now, James. It has been too long since I had such a fine ass to spill my seed into. I think I shall do this often. Unless you object," Peren remarked with a wicked grin.

"No! Do this -- all the time!" Justin found himself much less coherent.

His body was riding an upward wave of pleasure. Peren placed his hands on either side of Justin's head as he began to pump in short, strong strokes. Justin's body shook with the strength of the pounding he was getting. Waves of heat flowed out of his core and burst along his nerves. His whole body felt on fire. His cock and balls were filled with white-hot heat.

"Cum inside of me," Justin mewled

"Oh, gods, yes, you shall have my seed," Peren hissed.

His hips jabbed forward one last time, seating his cock fully within Justin's body. The boy arched and it seemed that Peren slipped in deeper as they both came. The hot spurts of cum inside of him made Justin's own orgasm more intense. He gripped onto Peren's back, his fingernails raking along the man's spine, as his own cock emptied against his belly. Peren's eyes closed and his body finally eased as the last spurt of semen left him.

Darkness plucked at the edges of Justin's vision. He could no longer control his limbs. He had no strength. Thankfully, Peren sank down beside him. The parting of his cock from Justin's hole made the boy moan his displeasure. But Peren spooned against him, soothing him.

As the older man's hot semen slowly dribbled out of his body, Peren whispered in his ear. "Sleep now, James, for soon you will have to be awake and aware. Those you thought loved you, those you trusted, will be at our doors with weapons of death and destruction, and we will have to defend ourselves against them once more."

Birth Rite

CHAPTER 7

ASHTARETH

*J*ustin awoke again, but this time it was to the sounds of chanting. It started off low and slow, but then the volume and tempo increased until it sounded as if a thousand souls were screaming into the dark pits of night. He jerked up. He didn't realize where he was at first. It looked to be a vast cave. Huge braziers were lit on either side of him and torches were placed intermittently on the tall stone walls.

The torch light illuminated the tips of huge stalactites hanging from the ceiling of the cave. Beneath his body was no longer the soft bed, but cold, hard stone. He gasped as he realized he was lying naked on a carved stone altar. The altar was on top of a raised platform in the center of this vast cavern. He couldn't see the far wall. The flickering torch light did not reach the far end of the cavern at all. Thick darkness clustered just outside of the glow of the torches. Stone stairs led up to the altar from a flat area twenty feet below him. There were over a dozen robed acolytes on their knees performing the chanting that had woken him.

Leading the group was another robed figure. This figure had on crimson robes instead of black. It was Peren. His platinum hair gleamed against the red material. His arms were outstretched. He radiated zeal in the strong lines of his back and the way his handsome head was tipped up, staring at the ceiling of the cavern.

But what they're praying to is down. Not up. Deep down, but stirring.

As if his thoughts alerted Peren to his wakefulness, the necromancer turned toward him. A beatific smile graced his face.

Am I to be sacrificed? Is that what the cost is to help Ellen?

Justin trembled. His tucked his slender limbs beneath him as he sought to jump up. But his strength drained away into the stone and he could only stare as Peren glided toward him.

"You awake on the Altar of Ashtareth!" Peren intoned. His silvery eyes gleamed.

"Why -- why are we here and -- and why am I ... naked?" Justin's lips trembled. The cave was cool, but it was fear that caused his trembling and not temperature.

"We are here to induct you as a true child of Ashtareth. You are nude, because you are being reborn, James. And a babe is always naked." Peren ran one pale hand down Justin's bare thigh. His other cupped the boy's cock and stroked it twice. "I believe you will enjoy the ceremony. It requires your beautiful body to be pierced by my cock once more."

Justin felt a stab of shame as his body reacted eagerly to the touches. His thighs parted slightly and Peren fingered his balls. The necromancer's hand then slid backward and Justin winced as his still-tender hole was touched. He couldn't help but imagine himself being taken on this foul altar while the acolytes chanted and the firelight gleamed on Peren's sweat-slicked body above him.

"Who are they?" Justin jerked his head toward the acolytes. He was now well aware that his slutishness was being seen by the hooded figures.

Peren released Justin's aching opening and covered his hands with the sleeves of his robe. "Townsfolk who saw things differently than the Devereauxs."

"People from Winter Haven?" The thought boggled Justin's mind. He couldn't imagine the people he saw every day like Sally the bus driver, or Al the mechanic, or Richard the doctor being amongst those that worshipped here.

"They are not all as pedestrian as you believe. Some you may even recognize." Peren's hands were back on Justin's body again, tweaking one of his nipples until the boy squirmed. His cock bobbed to fuller attention. "They understand how things truly are. Like you, they know the need to believe in things greater than what one can see."

Justin found himself leaning toward Peren as the man caressed his body. The necromancer kissed him deep and long, squeezing the base of Justin's cock until the boy moaned in pained pleasure.

"We can't have you cumming too soon. It will be so much better at the height of the ceremony when Ashtareth itself joins us and plunges its cock into your pretty pink mouth while I take you from behind," Peren explained.

Justin shuddered. What frightened him was that he wasn't sure whether it was in disgust or anticipation.

"After you have been inducted, you will be granted a robe such as mine. The knowledge of all Ashtareth's teachings will flow within you and you will truly be James LaMascares," Peren told him as he ran his thumb over Justin's swollen lips.

"And -- and Ellen? When do we bring her back?" Justin asked. He was doing this just to see her, to have her back alive. Without that he would not be here. He would have rejected all of Peren's advances and dark promises.

Or so he told himself.

Peren smile hugely. "Her soul is already here. She and my children await our call in the Outer Dark." He gestured toward the back of the cave that Justin could not see. The torch light abruptly stopped as if obstructed by a wall and only velvety darkness remained.

Ellen? Are you truly out there?

A wave of sweet rot rolled over him. Justin's tongue stuck to the top of his mouth. "Is the worm back there, too?"

"The Thyrumin squirms its way here. It will sway in time to our chants for Ashtareth. We shall be blessed with its unholy presence," Peren said.

This is insane, a part of Justin's mind screamed. *He just said unholy. UNHOLY! Is whatever he will have me do worth bringing Ellen back? Do I think she'll thank me for becoming a part of this unholy group?*

But I have to, another part of himself argued back. *Or she'll be gone forever. She'd do the same for me if the positions were reversed!*

No, she wouldn't! the first part cried. *Not because she doesn't love me, but because this is madness. She would know that unleashing Ashtareth and its followers upon the world is wrong and dangerous. I will be one of those followers. Will I enjoy it later? Like the blog writer?*

I can't stop them anyways, the defeatist part of him said. *So I might as well get Ellen back. Be on the side of the winners for once.*

She'll won't want to have anything to do with me! She'll be one of the people who will hunt me down! Justin realized.

Then he shook his head. He had no answer to his arguments on either side.

Peren's gaze suddenly fastened over his shoulder. An eager smile played upon his face. "Ah, they have arrived."

"What? Who?"

Justin wrenched his head over his shoulder to see where Peren was looking. There was a set of steps coming down from a high doorway carved out of the rock wall.

That's the way into the house, Justin guessed. *We're in the hill itself directly below it.*

His parents suddenly appeared in the doorway. The fact that Jack and Marie knew where to go confirmed Peren's story. They had killed the LaMascares. They had stolen him from his crib. He felt terribly treasured and sickened at the same time. He felt like he didn't know either sets of parents now.

Jack held a shotgun while his mother clutched a large silver cross. Justin gasped and tried to cover his erect cock as his parents' gaze found him. If only the shame he felt was a cloak on top of him. Peren let out a delighted laugh and grasped Justin's chin. He plundered the boy's mouth in front of his horrified parents. Justin struggled, but the addicting taste of the necromancer soon had him moaning and rubbing his body against Peren's with reckless abandon.

"You bastard!" Jack roared. He raised the shotgun.

"No, Jack, don't! You might hit Justin!" Marie cried out.

But her warning was too late. Justin heard the shotgun go off. His ears rang with the reverberations. He fully expected to feel the searing heat of buckshot in his chest. But it didn't happen. His eyes opened and he looked into Peren's silvery gaze. The necromancer was laughing. There wasn't a wound on either of them.

"Your puny weapons can do nothing against me!" Peren called out to them.

Marie's face had gone startlingly white while Jack's was blood red. Rage danced in Jack's eyes. Shock and horror, too.

"Get off of my son, you sick fuck!" Jack screamed.

"He is not your son!" Peren retorted hotly. "He is James LaMascares. My heir. The one who will bring about Ashtareth's reign on this Earth!"

What? I'm the one that brings Ashtareth? Not Peren? Me? No, no, no!

"Never!" Marie shouted. "Never! Justin, baby, fight him!"

"If you do then Ellen will remain a corpse in the Thyrumin's belly. Your best friend will walk in endless night. Her gifts lost from this world. Can you have that on your conscience?" Peren asked softly. "This is who you are, James."

"No, Justin! He's wrong!" Marie came down the stairs and raced onto the altar platform.

Peren raised a hand and she froze ten feet away. She tried to move forward, but it was as if she was glued in place. Her eyes showed her wild desire to get to him, but her body would not obey her. Jack ran down to her side, but he, too, suddenly became cemented in place. Peren laughed delightedly once more. His handsome face was lit from within by maliciousness.

Peren turned back toward him. "You will see them as I do soon, James. They are but food for the worms. If their bodies will not serve us willingly, we will make other uses of them."

The acolytes began to chant again. Justin felt a change in the air. A gust of nether wind suddenly entered the cave.

"There are passageways, countless tunnels, out there, James. I have not explored all their haunted depths. The Thyrumin guards those that lead down to Ashtareth itself and will not even let me pass," Peren explained as one of his arms fastened around Justin's shoulders while the other pointed into the vast darkness.

"It's coming, isn't it? Ashtareth is coming," Justin whispered.

The smell in the cave had changed. Though the rot of the worm richly tinted the breeze, there was a another smell, a colder smell like water that had never seen light, flowing below it.

"Yes, James. It is time. Ashtareth comes to us. Now get up on your hands and knees. Present yourself to me. The ceremony must begin!" Peren's voice rose in excitement.

Justin gave one last look at his parents. He wanted to help them, but it was like the will to do so wasn't there. He found himself twisting around and presenting himself like Peren requested. His cock quivered. Even his pucker throbbed with the knowledge that he would be fucked again.

And then the nightmare that is Ashtareth will come and make me suck from its cock. I'll do it, too. Probably eagerly. In front of my parents. In front of Ellen's soul.

Tears began to flow from Justin's eyes, landing on the top of the stone altar. The color of the stone changed as his salty tears rained down on it. The black stone gleamed and let off a blue light.

"Let our son go! Don't do this! He's just a boy!" Marie shouted.

"You'll pay for this, Peren! You scum! You bag of filth!" Jack screamed.

Justin's head dropped lower and he wept harder at his parents' words. They were going to die. He knew that. Peren wasn't going to allow them to live.

Their deaths are probably necessary to bring the others back, Justin realized. He shook at the knowledge. *What have I done? Oh, God, what have I done?*

"Ashtareth! Dark Father to us all! Hear our prayer! Come to see your newest child born into this world: James LaMascares!" Peren thundered.

The acolyte's chanting rose like a wave of sound. The air took on a more electric charge. Justin heard the rustle of Peren's robe opening. The necromancer was naked beneath it. His beautiful body glowed against the red silk. He was a vision of masculinity. His cock rose proudly from its nest of white curls, already slicked, and ready to pierce Justin.

"Look upon your beautiful boy who offers himself to you body and soul, Ashtareth. Let him be welcomed into your bosom!" Peren intoned.

Then the necromancer moved behind him. Justin tensed. His fingers dug into the stone altar as he expected to be speared on Peren's cock. But instead his head jerked up as he felt Peren's mouth on his ass instead. His anus trembled as the necromancer's tongue flickered against it. He moaned and spread his legs.

Why does it feel good? Must my debasement be pleasurable?

But his thoughts scattered as his body responded. He lowered his head to the cool surface of the altar, raising his ass further up for Peren's ministrations. The necromancer pulled apart his buttocks and his tongue delved deeply into Justin's back passage. The boy mewled as Peren's tongue stroked the silken walls of his insides. His cock was hard and leaking onto the altar. He felt his opening prepared only with Peren's spit. This fucking was going to be raw. There would be no horn to prepare the way now.

"Stop! Oh, God, STOP!" Jack shrieked.

Justin wanted to scream: no, don't stop, please, don't stop, Peren. Fuck me! Do it! He realized then that he *had* yelled those words out loud. He heard Marie begin the Lord's Prayer, but it was drowned out by the acolytes' frenzied chanting. The air was thick now like molasses. He could feel the power in it playing against his skin.

"I now will baptize you in Ashtareth's name by piercing your sweet body," Peren said. "Let this be done!"

Peren's cock was at his entrance and was sliding inside of him. Justin arched back into it. He was like a sheath for Peren's penis. Perfectly made to accept it. His body was on fire again. That spot inside of him throbbed.

"Fuck me! FUCK ME!" Justin screamed.

Peren grasped his hips and began to pound into him. Justin found himself skewering his ass backwards. He wished Peren's cock was bigger. He wanted to be filled more. Peren was chanting, his words alien yet familiar, as he fucked Justin. The acolytes were crying out in ecstasy. Something walked among them. The scent of blood rose up and frenzied screams mixed with choking shrieks of wonder. Ashtareth had granted some of its followers the joy of death.

"My seed is going to impart Ashtareth's grace within you! Oh, James, Ashtareth is here! The Dark Father is here! You are blessed! Blessed!" Peren called out.

Justin's balls drew tight to his body and his cock slapped against his stomach with each of Peren's thrusts. Pleasure and pain had taken his higher reason from him. He hardly cared that he was now a willing participant in this before his parents and Ellen's soul. He needed completion.

"Oh, my God, deliver our son from this evil! Please, I beg of you!" Marie's voice rose up above everything.

Justin thought he saw a golden glow coming from the cross she held in her hand, but his eyes were drawn away from her toward the winged being that now stood in front of him. Ashtareth was black as night. Its body gleamed like polished onyx. Its leathery wings stretched out behind it twenty feet or more. A long, curling tail tipped with bloody spikes thrashed around its clawed feet. Its head had a snout with sharp, black teeth and a lolling red tongue. Its eyes glimmered with unholy volcanic fire.

"Ashtareth! Oh, mighty Father!" Peren cried out. The pace of the fucking increased. The slap of his balls against Justin's upturned ass rose above all else.

Justin's eyes met Ashtareth's gaze and he was lost. The Dark Father grasped his chin in taloned hands and caressed his lips. The boy found himself opening his mouth and letting his tongue snake out. He tasted the god's skin. There was salt and something bitter like sulphur. That was when he saw the god's cock. It was seventeen inches long and black as pitch. Inside Justin screamed in terror. But only moans of desire left his lips. He opened his mouth wider, indicating that the god could have use of him.

No! What am I doing? NO!

But I have no choice. And I want this. I want to taste the semen of a god.

NO!

Ashtareth's cock rose and with one taloned hand it guided the head inside Justin's mouth. The taste on his tongue was acrid and sweet. He gagged as the being slowly, inexorably thrust the cock inside his mouth. It hit the back of his throat and Justin gagged again, but then it kept on going. He couldn't breathe, but Justin heard his own moans of pleasure. His cock was hot and hard, and his ass clenched down on Peren's cock as it tried to keep the necromancer's penis inside of him. He was filled completely.

Ashtareth's claws feathered in his hair as it began to thrust in and pull out in time with Peren's fucking. Justin sucked as much as he could on the god's penis. His stomach trembled as the first gush of cold precum dribbled down his throat and into it. Heat bloomed between his thighs. He was so aroused that his cock felt like it might explode. Ashtareth tipped its snout back and roared. The sound reverberated in the enclosed space.

"You are Ashtareth's child now, James! You will taste its seed and have mine in its name planted within your body," Peren yelled.

Peren thrust all the way in. His balls were pressed against Justin's opening. The boy felt the necromancer's cock begin to convulse as his semen burst forth. Justin's body lit up as Peren's cum sprayed inside of him. Ashtareth's cock quivered within him as it too began to pour its cum inside of his belly. Justin's orgasm reached its peak then, too. His semen drenched the stone altar.

Forgive me, Mom and Dad. Forgive me.

But suddenly the golden light that he had glimpsed before in his mother's hand was everywhere. Ashtareth screamed this time in pain and not pleasure. Its wings shredded as the golden light hit it. Peren wrenched around to face Marie who was now walking toward them, one hand outstretched, the cross glowing like it was on fire. It was her love for him, her belief in him.

Justin screamed, his mouth still around Ashtareth's cock as Peren wrenched his penis out of him. Semen and blood began to leak from his body. Peren tackled Marie. She went down hard. Her head struck the stone floor and the cross flew across the platform until it landed just below Justin's head. The light from it was extinguished.

James, I am James now. Not Justin, an alien voice said in his mind. *Justin Devereaux is dead.*

No, not yet I'm not.

Ashtareth pulled its penis out of him at that moment. It began to lumber toward his parents. Justin's body slumped down onto the altar. One of his arms was flung over the edge near the cross. There was the explosion of the shotgun. Peren and Ashtareth howled in rage, but not pain. Justin saw Peren's cloak flutter behind him as he ran toward Jack.

"Help me kill them, Dark Father! Help me add to your glory!" Peren screamed as his hands encircled Jack's throat. The remaining acolytes were streaming up the stairs to help in the slaughter. One of them raised a knife above Marie's prone body.

Justin reached for the cross. His fingers brushed along it. Strength pulsed up his arm. The cross glimmered slightly. He grasped the cross and the glow was back stronger than ever before. *No! What are you doing? You are James LaMascares! You worship Ashtareth! You wish this to happen!*

"My name is Justin Devereaux. And I want this stopped," Justin said.

He was suddenly able to get up to his feet. The light of the cross moved with him. Ashtareth's bulk, which was hovering above Marie, froze. It turned its snout toward him just as the glow reached its black form. The god screamed. Its onyx body began to flake away like ash in the wind. With a high-pitched wail it flapped its huge wings and took off from the platform and flew into the black depths.

"Some god you are," Justin's voice was hoarse.

The acolytes cowered before him. They screamed and covered their faces. It seemed that the light hurt them as well. Peren was the last to notice what was happening. He turned his head over his shoulder. His handsome face was marred by a scowl. He released Jack's throat and sent Justin's father hurtling to the ground. Jack groaned and flopped helplessly onto his side. Marie was still as stone as well. A bead of blood escaped her mouth.

Are they dead? No, God, no!

"What are you doing, James?" Peren asked.

"My name isn't James. It's Justin," Justin said as he took a step toward the necromancer.

"The god whose symbol you carry does not exist! Stop this foolishness!" Peren ordered. He stood unabashedly naked. His cock was covered with Justin's blood and was half-erect as if killing was just as exciting to him as fucking.

The glow of the cross didn't falter as Justin's face was unyielding. "It seems like it's real enough for Ashtareth. It left you here alone to face me."

Peren threw his head back and laughed. "It knew that I could best you in seconds. I do not wish to harm you, James. I am rather fond of you already." The lascivious smile he threw toward Justin had the boy's guts churning.

"My parents and I are leaving here."

"What about Ellen? Are you prepared to leave her spirit here forever?" Peren asked, eyebrows raising.

"Ellen isn't here or whatever part of her is, I release. She can go to wherever spirits go. I release you, Ellen!" Justin shouted.

"You have not the power to do that. James does, but you do not," Peren clucked.

The glow wavered as Justin grew afraid. *Is Ellen still here? Is she truly trapped here?*

76

Peren walked over to him, one hand outstretched. "Put that pathetic symbol away, James. It's time to become what you've always been meant to be. Ashtareth's emissary."

Justin thought he heard the flapping of obscene wings in the dark. He closed his eyes. He felt Peren's body heat against his own. The necromancer's lips suddenly parted over his. The kiss was almost sweet.

Forgive me, Ellen, if you are indeed still here. But I can't let this go on. I love you.

Peren screamed as the glow from the cross became blinding. Justin pressed the cross against the necromancer's forehead. The scent of burning flesh filled his nostrils. Peren's body blew apart in a wave of light and sound. Justin was sent spinning backward. His head slammed against the altar and he knew no more.

BIRTH RITE

CHAPTER 8

ALL'S WELL THAT ENDS...

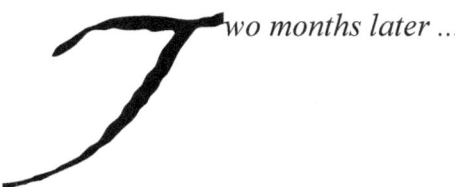*wo months later ...*

Justin put the last of his books on the bookshelf in his new room. He heard his mom call to his dad to bring her the box marked dishes.

"I refuse to eat on paper plates for our first meal in our new home!" she sang.

"I've found the plates, but not the silverware," Jack groused good-naturedly. "Can you bear to use plasticware?"

"I suppose so." Marie laughed.

Justin grinned. His parents sounded like their old selves again. Even though Marie's hair was streaked with gray and Jack's doctor was concerned that his normally hale and hearty physique had shrunk some.

They'll recover. They have to.

Justin stared down at the permanent burn scar across the palm that had held the cross. He grimaced slightly. His mother's hand did not bear the same mark. He worried it was there, because some part of him was still James LaMascares. He still had dreams of Peren's mouth on his, the older man's cock piercing him to his core, and he would wake with his belly drenched in his own semen. Shame filled him after those dreams, but a part of him still wanted to remember that impossible pleasure. He doubted he would ever truly experience it with anyone else.

His eyes glanced out his window. They had left Winter Haven and moved to another state. The LaMascares' Mansion was no longer a fixture out of his window. Instead he saw a prairie filled with tall grass and snow. But even if they had still been in Winter Haven, he wouldn't have been able to see the house on the hill anyway. It had burned down. His father and mother had ensured that. They had dragged him out, leaving the acolytes moaning in the dark and set the house on fire, trapping them within. Justin felt little pity for them. They had a choice: to burn or to go into the nighted tunnels of their god. He had a feeling that the flames would have been a better fate. Justin took in a deep breath and turned away from the view.

He still thought of Ellen often. Every day. He worried that some part of her was still in those nighted caverns beneath the LaMascares' Mansion. He didn't know how to find out if that was true or not. And if he somehow did discover that she was there, he wasn't sure what he could do about it.

Unless I embrace the James LaMascares' part of me and -- no! I won't do it! That path will only lead to bad things. I've got to believe Ellen is in heaven. Which is probably a lab for her. He smiled at the thought.

"Justin! Come down here and eat! The food is getting cold!" Marie called gaily.

"Coming, Mom!" Justin shouted back, relieved to be distracted from those dark thoughts.

He glanced at his computer's screen. The screensaver was not on. He frowned. He realized that a Word document was up. There was a few typed sentences on the otherwise blank document, *We have a long and glorious lineage stretching back before written history. We have survived in the dark, waiting until that fateful day we can raise the gods that are ours, to have the humans bow before us as they should. We are the elite! Forged in fires hotter than Hell. We came out like bright, sharp blades ready to cut down those that stand in our way! We are born rulers. The rest are cattle.*

Hands shaking and forehead dotted with cold sweat, Justin quickly deleted the words he didn't recall typing. He then shut his computer down altogether and stared at it with trembling lips.

"Justin! Your father is going to eat your share if you don't get down here right away!" his mother called again with a laugh.

Justin loped down the stairs and into the kitchen. He tried to school his expression into one of normalness even as he wondered about the other blog writer whose words he had copied upstairs unconsciously. Had they killed themselves? Had they surrendered to the LaMascares' part of themselves? And what about the other children?

His parents had admitted there had been over a dozen children taken away from the mansion just as they had taken him. They claimed not to know where the kids all were. He wasn't sure if he believed them. There was sometimes a worried, calculating light in his parents' eyes. Maybe they wondered if he was still James LaMascares, too, in some small corner of his brain. But surely with

Peren gone all of the darkness would be gone, too, from the LaMascares line. Or so he hoped. So he prayed.

"There he is! Come on! Sit on down and dig in. Your mother made some mean fried chicken and potatoes," Jack said from his spot at the Formica covered table.

Jack patted the spot beside him. Justin walked over and sat down next to his father. He had feared that Jack would reject him after what he had seen Justin do on the altar, especially when weeks afterward, Justin had confessed to being gay. It seemed a small thing after everything. But it had still felt huge. Jack had merely held him and said he loved him. Simple as that

Marie sat down as she set a plate loaded with food in front of Justin, breaking him out of his memories. The smell of warm chicken wafted up to Justin's nose. He drew in a deep breath and grimaced.

"What's wrong, honey?" Marie asked.

Justin felt a tremor go through him as he took in another breath. He smelled rot. Sweet rot. "Nothing, Mom. Just thought I --"

"Oh, goodness, that door is open again, Jack! I thought you said you fixed it," Marie said.

The door she was talking about was to the basement. It opened into the kitchen. The moldy scent that Justin had smelled was coming from there. His shoulders slumped. It was just the basement in their new house. Nothing more. Jack got up and shut the door firmly.

"Must be the catch that causes it to keep opening up. I'm sure that's all," Jack said.

"Well, I want you to really fix it. We've got to do something about that smell, too. The last owners said they had some problems with a leaky foundation," Marie said.

"Cracks in the foundation?" Justin asked. His hand with the fork froze halfway up to his mouth from the plate. He had never told his parents exactly what had happened to Ellen and her family. They hadn't asked either, as if they were afraid to know.

"I think so. A portion of the wall is bowed inward. We'll have to hire someone to fix that right away," Marie said absently.

Justin swallowed hard. He slowly lowered the fork to the plate before he turned his gaze toward the basement door. He watched as the catch gave way again. The door opened slowly, only an inch or two, as if someone was standing there had cracked it open to watch them from the darkness below.

"Is anything wrong, honey?" Marie asked, catching his gaze.

He stared at the slice of darkness. He thought he heard the barest sound of fabric rustling. Someone could be there. Peren could be there. Peren would follow him to the ends of the earth. And if he wanted to let Peren back into his life, he could. Peren would kiss him and fuck him again. Make him moan once more with forbidden pleasure and pain while whispering secrets of the old gods in his ears. All would be forgiven. His parents thought it was over and done. But Justin knew better. It would never be over until he was dead and perhaps not even then. He was a LaMascares after all, and death was more an obstacle than an end.

He swallowed down the bile -- and excitement -- that rose up in his throat. Then he looked at his parents. He needed their strength to help him resist the darkness inside of him. He opened his mouth tell them what he feared, but he found himself saying instead, "No, nothing at all."

The End?

PUBLISHING

<u>Raythe Reign Deals & Coupons</u>

Are you in the mood for more dark, sexy m/m stories? Check out our online shop here, where you can find ALL available works from us (some not available on Amazon.)

http://shop.raythereign.com

And if you want to be the first to know about new Raythe Reign releases, join our update list!

We'll send you a note as soon as the next volume is out. People on our update list will also get some insider info...

- <u>Exclusive monthly deals</u> for books and manga through our own shop.
- Coupons for our monthly membership, which has *something new to see or read* every day of the year (even Christmas!)
- Contests, giveaways, and things like AMAs (ask-me-anything sessions.)
- Events we're participating in, such as conventions, discussion panels, etc.
- Progress updates about current series, new series, stories, and side content.

- Exclusive content you can ONLY find through our shop, such as sexy stories and graphic novels that are <u>too hot for Amazon</u> to sell.

Join here: http://shop.raythereign.com/raythe-reign-update-list/

- Raythe Reign Team

www.ingramcontent.com/pod-product-compliance
Lightning Source LLC
Chambersburg PA
CBHW060047150626
46556CB00018BA/3106